ANIMAL
RESCUE

Holly

This series is for my riding friend
Shelley, who cares about all animals.

ISBN-13: 978-0-545-16630-0
ISBN-10: 0-545-16630-6

Text copyright © 2008 by Jenny Oldfield
Illustrations copyright © 2008 by Sharon Rentta
Cover illustration copyright © 2008 by Simon Mendez

12 11 10 9 8 7 6 5 4 3 2   9 10 11 12 13 14/0

Printed in the U.S.A.
First Scholastic printing, December 2009

Holly

Tina Nolan
Illustrated by Sharon Rentta

SCHOLASTIC INC.

New York   Toronto   London   Auckland
Sydney   Mexico City   New Delhi   Hong Kong

ANIMAL MAGIC
Meet the animals

Visit our website at
www.animalmagicrescue.net

Working our
magic to match
the perfect pet
with the perfect
owner!

LOTTIE

Lottie would love a warm
home and a family of her
own. Can you give her the
care she needs?

BUFFY

Buffy is a lap cat. Curl up
for lots of cozy nights with
this gorgeous girl—
purrfect!

FLASH

A sweet cat with big paws!
Flash loves the outdoors.
He needs a big yard away
from main roads.

RESCUE CENTER
in need of a home!

SASHA AND RUBY

Two fluffy youngsters who need a home together. Are you willing to comb and cuddle them?

CHARLIE

A lively boy, good with children. Recovering from an operation, so needs plenty of TLC.

BRUNO

Don't let his tough act fool you—Bruno's the shy, reserved type who will follow wherever you go.

MAX

Max's elderly owner has been taken into the hospital. Can you give him a new home?

Chapter One

"Karl, come and look at this!" On the Monday before Christmas, Eva Harrison called her brother into the yard at Animal Magic Rescue Center.

Karl stuck his head out of the stable block. "I can't right now. I've got to finish mucking out Rosie's stable."

"It will only take a minute. Just come and look at this puppy playing with the yard broom." Eva couldn't help laughing. The tiny black-and-white Border collie had clamped her jaws onto the bristles and was growling and tugging the whole thing into the middle of the frosty yard. "She thinks she's really tough!"

"Yap!" The pup wriggled and rolled, covering herself in white frost and almost whacking herself with the broom handle.

Though he was busy mucking out, Karl came to have a look. "Who does she belong to?"

"Mr. Price brought her in with three other puppies. Mom has given them their first set of shots. This one made a run for it. You're an escapee, aren't you?" Eva said, crouching down and stroking the pup. "But you're very, *very* cute."

"Not bad," Karl said, picking the puppy up and dusting her off. "We can find a home for you, no problem. And your brothers and sisters, too."

The lively pup licked Karl's hand and wriggled free. Once more, she stalked the broom, then pounced. "Yip-yap-yap!"

"Adorable!" Eva sighed. It was one of her dreams to have a puppy of her own, but her mom and dad had a strict rule about not adopting any of the pets who came into the center.

"Come back here, you little rascal!" a voice called from the doorway into the waiting room. It was the puppy's owner, Joe Price, who lived up at Moorview Farm.

At last Eva persuaded the puppy to let go of the broom. She carried her across to the farmer. "What's her name?" Eva asked, handing the pup over.

"This one is named Holly." The farmer half smiled as he grasped the wriggling puppy. "There's one other girl in the litter. She's called Ivy. Holly and Ivy—Christmas puppies, get it?" A huge grin spread across his face. "The boys are Bill and Ben."

"Holly, Ivy, Bill, and Ben," Karl repeated the names. "Would you like us to put them on the Animal Magic website?"

Joe Price shook his head. "No need for that. I'm hoping to turn three of these pups into working dogs. Bill is going to Adam Ingleby over at High Trees."

"We know Adam," Eva broke in. "He helped us set up a hedgehog sanctuary in the woods behind the farm."

The farmer nodded in response. "Ivy will stay with me, and Ben is going to my cousin's sheep farm up north. He has a farm near Gretna and is planning to train Ben for top-level sheepdog trials."

Eva and Karl followed Joe back into the waiting room where their mom, Heidi Harrison, and the vet's assistant, Jen, were entering the pups' details in the computer.

"And what about Holly?" Eva smiled wistfully as her favorite of the four pups refused to go back into Joe's well-used pet carrier.

"Yip!" Holly cried, climbing out of the carrier and launching herself from the desk onto the floor.

Karl lunged at her, but Holly was too quick. She scooted under the magazine rack and hid under the bench in the waiting area.

"She's a live wire, this one." Joe chuckled.

"And she's probably the brightest of the bunch. But she's not going to be put to work. I've sold her to a woman who stopped at the farm the other day to buy a Christmas holly wreath. Her name's Andrea Waterson. She lives somewhere in town. To be honest, I don't know much more than that about her." Joe looked at his watch and realized he had to go. "Holly's clever, so I hope the Watersons take her to dog-training classes—otherwise she could be quite a handful!"

While Karl went after Holly, Eva fired questions at the farmer. "Have you told Mrs. Waterson about training Holly properly? Does she have a nice big yard? Does she realize that dogs need at least two good walks a day?"

"Whooaa!" Joe begged, grinning at Heidi Harrison and holding up his hands in mock surrender.

"Sorry about my daughter giving you the third degree, Joe," Heidi broke in with an apologetic smile. "Eva worries about every creature in the entire world!"

Joe nodded. "I must admit, I wasn't that happy about selling Holly to Mrs. Waterson," he muttered. "But she offered me a good price and I accepted."

"I know, Joe. Times are hard for farmers these days," Heidi sympathized. "You have to earn money where you can."

"Come on, let's get you back into the carrier," Karl said to Holly as he cornered her under the bench and picked her up. This time Holly didn't struggle as he stroked her, then snuggled her in beside her sister and brothers.

"Remind me—are the puppies fully weaned?" Jen asked Joe for her records.

"Yes. They're eight weeks old and their mom's just about had enough of them," Joe replied. "They're on solid food three times a day."

"And we've given you dewormers for them, plus they've had their antiflea treatment along with everything else." Jen saved the updated file before closing the screen. "That's everything, then. They're ready to face the big wide world. I can print out vaccination certificates and send them to you in the next couple of days."

"Great. That means I can let the new owners know that they can pick them up before Christmas." The farmer closed the carrier and lifted it up. The puppies yapped and scrambled inside.

"Good luck!" Heidi called after him, raising her eyebrows at Eva as Joe crossed the frosty yard. "Don't even think about it!"

"What?" Eva faked ignorance.

"I know you, Eva! Don't think about running after Joe and quizzing him again about Holly's new owner!"

"B-b-but . . . !" Eva hadn't liked the sound of Mrs. Waterson—the woman who'd gone to Moorview to buy a holly wreath, but ended up walking away with a puppy as well. "What if she doesn't know anything about how to look after a dog?"

"Your worries might well be justified," her mom said firmly, watching the farmer put the pet carrier into his Land Rover and drive off. "But it's none of our business, Eva. There's nothing we can do."

Chapter Two

As Joe Price drove out of Animal Magic with his four adorable pups, Eva and Karl's dad drove in. He jumped out of his delivery van and ran around to the back door. "Can you give me a hand with this cat?" he yelled. "Careful you don't slip on the ice!"

"Go get a carrier," Heidi told Karl as she and Eva rushed over to the van.

"I'm sure she's a stray. I found her in the empty lot at the back of the post office,"

Mark Harrison explained as he eased open the door. "That lot is pretty much deserted at this time of year—no one really goes out there once the weather changes. The poor creature had been forced to make a den next to some trash cans. I expect she'd have frozen to death if she'd stayed out much longer."

Heidi nodded. "They're forecasting twenty-five degrees tonight. And I doubt she's had anything to eat lately."

"Poor thing!" Eva cried as her mom reached in and took hold of the stray.

The female cat was a mixture of brown, black, and dirty white. Hardly more than skin and bone, she looked as if she'd given in and was ready to die.

Karl reappeared with the carrier and his mom gently lowered the patient in and rushed back to the exam room.

"Eva, get a blanket to wrap her in," her mom ordered. "We need to restore her body temperature and rehydrate her as quickly as we can. Jen, we'll need to hook her up to an IV." Quickly, Dr. Harrison took control, fighting to save the cat, who lay on her side without moving. "Somebody give her a name," she suggested.

"Lottie!" The name came to Eva right away. "Because she was found in an empty lot."

"Okay, Lottie, you'll feel a small prick," Heidi said gently as she inserted the needle to connect her to the IV. "Jen and I are going to take you next door into the cat kennels and put you under a nice heat lamp. When you're feeling better, we'll give you a more thorough exam."

The cat blinked and took a deep breath. She didn't raise her head as she was carried next door.

"I'll start on her website entry," Karl decided, typing some words into a blank document. "Lottie would love a warm home and a family of her own. Can you give her the care she needs?"

"Yes, that's good. But don't put it up on the site yet," his mom advised.

"I feel so sorry for her," Eva murmured. "Let's just hope that Dad found her in time." Then she remembered something. "Hey, Karl, did you close the stable door when you came out to see Holly?"

"Uh-oh! I don't think I did."

Karl and Eva dashed out into the yard, just in time to see Rosie taking advantage of the open door. The shaggy little Shetland pony ventured out into the yard, closely followed by Merlin.

"Stop!" Eva cried, waving her arms and trying to shoo Rosie and Merlin back the way they'd come.

The Shetland and the gray foal slid and skidded on the icy surface while Merlin's mother, Guinevere, stuck her head over the stable door and whinnied.

"That's right, Gwinnie—you tell them to stop messing around!" Eva muttered, grabbing Rosie's bridle and turning her around. "Uh-oh, here comes Annie!"

Sure enough, her neighbor Annie Brooks had been out in her driveway and had heard the clatter of hooves. She and her mom were boarding Guinevere, Merlin, and Rosie at Animal Magic until their new stables were finished. "What's going on?" she asked.

"Nothing. It's okay. Karl and I were just about to take these three out into the field to save you the trouble." Eva tried to make it sound as if everything was under control but naughty Rosie was making it difficult.

"They'll need their blankets," Annie decided, fetching them from the tack room. "Mom and Dad are out in the field. Dad's taken time off from work to finish building the stables. He says they should be ready by Christmas. Mom wants to have a party to celebrate—maybe for New Year's."

"Cool!" Quickly Eva and Annie put on Rosie's and Merlin's winter blankets while Karl fastened a halter on Guinevere. Soon they were all on their way to the Brookses' field.

"Hey, Gwinnie, look at that!" Karl exclaimed when he saw Annie's parents hard at work on the wooden stables. "That's a five-star accommodation for horses!"

Jason Brooks looked up from his hammering. "Hi there!" he called.

"They look amazing," Eva said, letting Rosie go and walking up the hill to inspect the stable block. "The horses are going to love it!"

"And you and Karl will no doubt be glad not to have to muck them out at your place." Linda Brooks handed her husband another handful of nails, then stood back to admire their work. "They'll be off your hands for good."

"We've loved having them stay," Eva protested. "We're going to miss them."

"Well, feel free to come and muck out here as often as you like!" Mr. Brooks grinned.

"Will do!" Eva smiled back. It was time to go. There was still a ton of stuff to do, including checking on Lottie and putting up a Christmas tree. "Better go!" she said. "See you later!"

Chapter Three

"How's Lottie?" Eva asked Jen as she followed Karl into the exam room.

"She's doing okay," Jen replied. "But it's early still. Your mom thinks we should wait a while longer before putting her up on the website."

Eva frowned. "That doesn't sound good."

"She's been through a lot," Jen reminded her. "Keep your fingers crossed that she'll pull through."

"Hey, we've got an e-mail from Joel!" Karl

announced as he logged on and caught up with the rescue center messages.

Joel had worked as Dr. Harrison's assistant before Jen. Now he was in Russia, working on a big cattle ranch on the frozen tundra.

"What does he say?" Eva asked.

"Merry Christmas, and he hopes we all have a great time," Karl reported. "He says he plans to be back in England for New Year's Eve."

"Cool!" Eva watched Jen open the flaps of a cardboard box and pick up a pale brown rabbit with floppy ears.

"Luckily, there's nothing wrong with young Sasha here, except that her ex-owners think she's too much trouble," Jen commented.

Tutting, Eva went to stroke Sasha. She peered into the box. "Who's this?" she asked, gazing at the matching rabbit still in there.

"That's Ruby, Sasha's sister. She's got darker tips on her ears—see."

"Sasha and Ruby," Eva murmured. "What did the owners say?"

"Not much. Just that the family was going away for Christmas and they couldn't find anyone to look after the rabbits. Plus, they've had them for six months and the kids were supposed to groom them and look after them, but they never bothered, so that's how they ended up here."

"Right!" Eva went straight to the computer and found the Animal Magic Newcomers file. "Sasha and Ruby," she typed. "Two fluffy youngsters who need a home together. Are you willing to comb and cuddle them?"

"How does that sound?" she asked her mom, who had just come in from the kennels.

"Perfect. Karl's already taken their photo.

It's very sweet. Before you know it, there'll be a line of people wanting to adopt them."

"We hope!" Quickly, Eva clicked through the list of animals on their website. There was Charlie, the lively collie mix, and Max, the overweight Jack Russell whose owner had gone into the hospital. Plus Buffy, the pretty black cat with pale gray eyes, and Flash, the outdoor orange tomcat who only came home to eat. On and on the list went. But not many rabbits, Eva noticed, so they stood a good chance of a quick adoption. Then again, perhaps it would be better for Ruby and Sasha not to be adopted before Christmas, she thought. After all, the saying that a dog was for life, not just for Christmas, applied to rabbits, too.

Just then, the door opened and Eva's dad staggered in, carrying a tall Christmas tree. "Make way!" he gasped as Eva rushed to hold open the door. "Where do you want this?" he asked Heidi.

"Over by the window, beside the magazine rack," Heidi said, clearing a path.

"Granddad chose it and dug it up and put it in a pot especially for us," her dad told them. "He says we're late getting ourselves organized and this was the best one left in the whole garden center."

"You can smell the pine needles!" Eva loved the buildup to Christmas—finding the box of decorations in the attic, checking if the lights still worked, straightening the silver wings of the angel that perched on top of the tree. "When can we decorate it?" she asked eagerly.

"After office hours," her mom insisted as the door opened again and another patient came in—an elderly golden retriever who needed to have some teeth taken out. "Hello, Mr. Frears. Bring Penny this way!"

"Busy, busy!" Eva's dad straightened up and eased his back. "It's always like this just before Christmas—people suddenly deciding that they can't cope with their pets."

"Yes, I remember last year," Eva said, standing back to admire the tall, straight tree. She tried not to think too much about careless owners who abandoned their animals, and instead looked ahead to tonight—to trimming the tree and wrapping the presents she'd bought for her mom, her dad, and Karl. "I love Christmas. It's so great!" She sighed. "And there's only four days to go!"

Chapter Four

"This time next week, it'll all be over," Jen said matter-of-factly as Mr. Harrison dropped her off at the train station early the next morning. It was three days before Christmas and Jen was traveling home to her family in Ireland for the holiday break.

The town was decorated with giant stars, angels, and Santas. The streets were crowded with last-minute shoppers.

"I know—is it worth it?" Mark said with a grin. "We all spend too much, eat too much, expect too much . . . bah humbug!"

"You old Scrooge!" Eva protested. "I bet you used to love Christmas when you were my age, way back in the olden days!"

"Watch it!" Mark laughed as he helped Jen with her suitcase. "Have a great time and see you next week."

Jen gave Eva a hug. "Don't forget to drop off those vaccination certificates at Joe Price's place on your way back," she reminded her. "They're in the glove compartment. He's arranged for the pups to be picked up today, so he needs them in a hurry."

"I won't forget," Eva promised. She waved good-bye to Jen as her dad turned his van around. "That means you'll get to meet Mr. Price's four adorable puppies," she said eagerly. "There's Bill and Ben, plus Holly and Ivy. They're all going to be working dogs except Holly."

Over the past twenty-four hours, Eva had been too busy to think much about the cute Border collie pups. But now she told her dad all about them as they drove out of town back to Okeham. "Adam Ingleby is going to take Bill. Ben's going to be trained to do sheepdog trials like the ones you see on TV. That's what I'd do if I was allowed to have a collie pup." She said this slowly to make sure her dad paid attention, but she got no response. "They're so clever, they can learn any trick you teach them—they can do obstacle courses through plastic tunnels and over fences and little wooden bridges."

"They're definitely great dogs," her dad agreed.

"And Holly is the best of all. She's got the cutest black-and-white face, with big brown eyes. Her ears kind of fold and flap forward over her face, like someone did origami on them. And her front paws are white with tiny gray speckles—"

"Whoa!" Her dad laughed as he took an icy back road up toward Moorview Farm. "I was wondering why you'd left Lottie and offered to drive into town with me and Jen. Now I know it was because you've fallen seriously in love with one of Joe Price's pups!"

Eva sniffed. "Maybe," she admitted. "But honestly, Dad—Holly is so-o-o cute!"

"How *is* Lottie, by the way?" he asked, changing the subject and turning carefully into the lane up to the farm.

"Much better this morning. Mom had to cut some of the knots out of her fur, so she looks scrawny now. But she's a lot stronger. She can stand up while you gently brush her. And she loves being stroked."

"That all sounds good," her dad said, parking his van and leaping out. Eva collected the certificates from the glove compartment and followed her father across the farmyard.

"Hello!" Eva said to a wary gray-and-white collie who came out of one of the barns to greet them, closely followed by Joe Price.

The dog wagged her bushy tail in response to Eva's voice.

"This is Jess," Mr. Price told them. "She's the puppies' mother, and a good old girl. Aren't you, dear? This is her third litter."

"We've just come to drop off the pups' vaccination records," Mark explained, handing over the paperwork as Eva made a fuss over Jess.

"Can Dad see the puppies?" she asked the farmer, dying to take a peek herself.

"Feel free. They're in the barn, in one of the old cow stalls. You can't miss them."

Eva led her dad into the dark, dusty stone barn, following the sound of lively yapping until they came to a straw-lined stall where Holly, Ivy, Bill, and Ben romped and wrestled happily.

"Aren't they adorable?" Eva murmured. She picked out the two male puppies— already bigger and broader than their sisters. Then she pointed to Ivy. "Mr. Price is going to keep her," she explained.

"So this one is Holly?" her dad asked, as the fourth pup ran to the door and jumped up as if she were on springs. "Look—she thinks you're here to play."

Eva laughed. "She played hide-and-seek in the waiting room the other day—that was after she'd wrestled with the broom!"

"I can see why she's your favorite," her dad admitted. "Look at that face—you'd swear she's listening to every word we say!"

Just then Mr. Price appeared in the doorway. "Mrs. Waterson's here to get Holly," he told Eva and her dad. "Can you grab her, Eva?"

With a deep sigh, Eva opened the stall door and slipped inside. Little Holly ran straight over to her and jumped up again. "Hi, Holly. You're coming with me," Eva said quietly. She felt sad as she picked her up.

"Say good-bye to your brothers and sister," she whispered.

The puppies yipped and yapped as Eva carried Holly out. "Time to go," she said, sighing again.

"Thank you for calling to tell me that the puppy was ready," Mrs. Waterson said to Joe Price out in the farmyard. She spoke so fast, it was hard to hear what she was saying. "I'm on my way to drop Lulu off at the kennel and was passing this way."

Still carrying Holly in her arms, Eva paused at the barn door. Mrs. Waterson wasn't what she'd pictured. Not that she really knew what she'd been expecting. In person, Holly's new owner was a small, dainty woman in fancy trousers and high heels.

"Ah, there you are, Holly!" Mrs. Waterson exclaimed, turning toward the barn. "Come here, sweetie. We're going to take you home!"

Who's we? Eva wondered, before spotting a small boy sitting in the large station wagon parked beside her dad's van. Then she noticed that he wasn't alone. Beside him sat a huge gray Great Dane!

"Todd can't wait to get Holly home," Mrs. Waterson told Joe Price. "I promised he could have a puppy as an early Christmas present if he did well on his school exams. Luckily, he got A's in most of his subjects, so here we are!"

Eva pursed her lips. "Good for Todd!" she muttered under her breath. "What's the Great Dane called?" she asked out loud.

"That's Lulu. She's really Gina's—Todd's sister's—dog." Mrs. Waterson seemed determined to give them the full family history. "Gina has gone with her father to our house in Spain for Christmas, which is why we're putting Lulu in the kennel because she's too much of a handful for me and Todd to cope with by ourselves."

Eva wondered why Todd didn't look very

cheerful as he sat in the car, staring out at his new puppy. In fact, he seemed to be definitely *un*-cheerful, sitting beside a dog bigger than he was. The Great Dane seemed equally unhappy.

"Todd, come and look!" Mrs. Waterson called her son from the car. Todd opened the door and stepped out slowly. He was about eight, with dark hair like his mom's, and wearing jeans and new sneakers. "He's not used to the countryside," his mother explained to Joe Price and Eva. "He's a bit nervous around farm animals."

"Remember not to spoil the puppy," Mr. Price warned as he gave Mrs. Waterson Holly's certificate. "And you, too, Todd," he added as, with a nervous smile, the boy took Holly from the farmer. "No treats from the table. No sleeping at the foot of your bed. Otherwise she'll be spoiled rotten."

"Just like Lulu!" said Mrs. Waterson. "I'm always warning Gina that she spoils her!"

The down-to-earth farmer gave Mrs. Waterson a sharp look as if he was having more second thoughts about selling Holly to her. But he was quickly distracted by another car turning into the yard. It was Adam Ingleby from High Trees.

"Merry Christmas, Adam!" Eva's dad called. "Have you come for your pup, too?"

A nod from Adam sent Eva running into the barn to get Bill. "Down, Ben. Down, Ivy!" she insisted, reaching for Bill. She closed the stall door and ran back to the yard, clutching the wriggling puppy.

Meanwhile, Mrs. Waterson chose that precise moment to get her pet carrier from the car. Lulu seized her chance; she leaped out and broke into a galloping run toward Todd, jumping up and almost knocking him clean over.

"Watch out, Lulu!" Todd cried as he overbalanced and dropped Holly.

"Lulu, come back!" Mrs. Waterson wailed.

Little Holly rolled clear of Lulu and Todd, then raced toward Eva and Bill. "Yip!

Yap!" The excited brother and sister were reunited.

"I couldn't help it!" Todd blurted out before his mom had chance to yell.

By this time, Lulu, Bill, and Holly were running wild in the yard, with steady old Jess looking on calmly from the barn.

"I'm so sorry about this," Mrs. Waterson said in a helpless, exasperated voice. "Oh, dear, now I'm going to have a terrible time getting Lulu into the car."

"She's not vicious, is she?" Adam asked, preparing to separate his puppy from Holly and Lulu.

"Not in the least. She wouldn't hurt a fly. But unfortunately, my husband is the only one she listens to. I can't get her to do a thing I tell her. Todd, you pick Holly up. If we get her in the car first, maybe Lulu will follow."

Eva watched Todd and Adam rescue their pups and carry them to their cars. Meanwhile, Eva's dad and Joe decided to try to grab hold of Lulu.

"This isn't a game!" Mark exclaimed as Lulu turned to lick his face with her long, slobbery tongue. He took her by the collar and held tight. Slowly but firmly, he led the Great Dane to the Watersons' car. "Wow, she's almost as big as Linda's Shetland pony!"

Joe Price shook his head as the mother and son jumped in after Lulu and quickly drove off. "I only hope I've done the right thing," he muttered.

"Well, at least you can trust me—I'll take good care of Bill," Adam promised, pocketing his puppy's certificate and wishing them all Merry Christmas before he drove off.

Eva stood for a long time in the almost empty farmyard. "But honestly, how will Holly cope with having to share a home with Lulu?" she said, though she hardly expected an answer. "And what chance is there of the Watersons taking good care of *her*?"

Chapter Five

"If you were named Eve, not Eva, tomorrow we could all say, 'It's Christmas Eve, Eve!'"

It was two days before Christmas and Eva's granddad, Jimmy Harrison, made his annual family joke. He sat in the kitchen at Animal Magic drinking coffee and eating pie.

"Ha-ha, Granddad!" Eva wrinkled her nose. "Isn't it time you made up a new joke? Anyway, come see the Christmas tree in the office. Karl and I decorated it the day before yesterday. It's cool!"

"Okay, I'm coming, but don't pull me over!" Her grandfather let himself be tugged by the hand.

Eva crossed the slippery yard with him, then opened the door to the office. Jimmy Harrison stared up at the tree. "Good lord, that's certainly stunning!"

Covered in tiny white lights and draped with silver balls, with the angel perched precariously on top, the tree took up half the space in the waiting area.

"You chose it for us," Karl reminded his granddad from over at the computer. Then he turned to his mom. "Can I put Lottie up on the website yet?"

"Let's wait till after Christmas," she advised. "She's doing well, but I want to keep her here for at least a week so I can make sure there aren't any complications from her hypothermia. And by the way, Eva, have you checked on Penny this morning?"

Eva nodded. "I went into the kennels before breakfast. She's still tired, but otherwise she seems okay."

"Penny was brought in for dental treatment," Heidi explained to Granddad. "But while I was examining her, her owner, Mr. Frears, mentioned a bladder problem, and it didn't take me long to diagnose a bladder stone. I operated right away and removed a stone as big as a peach."

"Ouch!" Karl muttered.

"Poor Penny. It must have really hurt." Glancing over her brother's shoulder, Eva saw that he had booked an appointment for a Mr. and Mrs. Jackman to come see Ruby and Sasha. "What did the Jackmans sound like?" she asked.

"Good. They breed rabbits and are looking for some more flop-eared females. They're coming in this morning at eleven," he reported. "I'm going to spruce the rabbits up. Do you want to help?"

"Listen," Granddad cut in. "I can see you're all pretty busy here. Maybe I'll skip the rest of that coffee and come back later."

"No way, Granddad! We're never too busy for you." Eva grabbed him again and led him back across the yard toward the house.

"Dad, can you heat up Granddad's coffee?" she yelled. "And if you pour one for Mom I'll take it back out!"

The Jackmans came at eleven and fell in love with Ruby and Sasha. They took them away in a brand-new pet carrier, promising to give the pretty rabbits a fresh start in a loving home. At lunchtime, Mr. Frears visited Penny and was relieved to see that his faithful girl was well on the road to recovery. Soon afterward, Karl and Eva took two dogs from the kennels on a walk.

Pixie was a tiny whippet mix who loved to run off the leash, so Eva let her loose. Bruno was the opposite—a burly but timid boxer who stayed close to Karl's side.

As they walked by the river, examining the thin layer of ice at the water's edge and wondering happily about the presents they would soon be opening, Annie ran down the field toward them, waving. "Hey, you two!" she began. "Guess what—it's going to snow!"

"Says who?" Karl asked, bending down to give Bruno a reassuring pat.

The boxer trembled as Gwinnie cantered

down after Annie, her big hooves thudding over the frozen ground. Rosie and Merlin followed more slowly.

"Mom heard it on the weather forecast. It's going to be a white Christmas. And guess what else!"

"Something good?" Eva guessed from her friend's excited expression.

Annie nodded. "Dad's finally finished the stables! Gwinnie, Merlin, and Rosie can spend their first night there tonight!"

As if she understood, Gwinnie threw back her head and whinnied.

"Wow, that's cool!" Eva tried not to show that she was sad. "I'll bring their stuff over from our place as soon as I've finished walking Pixie."

"I'll come over and help you," Annie promised. She pulled her red knitted hat farther down her forehead to keep out the biting wind.

"Mom says you can have some special food supplements for Merlin that she's got in her storeroom," Eva said. "It's his first winter, so he's bound to feel the cold."

"Thanks, Eva." Annie leaned over the fence, suddenly serious. "I mean, really— thanks for everything you've done for

Gwinnie and Merlin—and Rosie!"

Eva gulped back some sudden tears. She was going to miss the horses at Animal Magic! "No problem," she muttered, turning to call Pixie.

"Mom and I will really, *really* look after them," Annie promised. "And you can come and see them anytime you want!"

"Twenty-three degrees!" Karl checked the thermometer on the porch.

A starlit night and a frosty morning had passed since the horses had gone to their new stable. It was late afternoon on Christmas Eve and the faint winter sun had already set. Frost sparkled on the roof and the cobbled yard.

Eva stopped sweeping out the empty stables and peered over the door. "Easily cold enough for snow!" she commented hopefully. A white Christmas would be perfect.

The daily jobs at the rescue center were done—dogs walked, cats fed, small animal cages cleaned—and Dr. Harrison was finishing up in the exam room when Eva recognized Adam Ingleby's old red Land

Rover as it pulled up in the yard.

"What does he want at this time on Christmas Eve?" she wondered. "Maybe he ran out of puppy food and the stores all closed early."

"Hi, Adam!" Karl waved. "What's wrong?"

"It's Bill. Is your mother around?" Adam asked, hurriedly carrying his limp and seemingly lifeless puppy towards the office.

"I'm here," Eva's mom assured him, popping her head around the open door, beckoning him inside.

Eva and Karl ran to join them.

"There's something wrong with Bill," Adam told the vet. "The first thing I noticed was last night—he didn't eat his food. I didn't think too much of it at first—I figured it was a delayed reaction to his vaccinations. Then this morning I noticed he had the sniffles."

"Let's take a look," Dr. Harrison said, carrying Bill into the examination room. She felt his stomach and peered into his mouth, then took his temperature.

"Not good, is it?" Adam guessed.

"His temperature's sky high," she answered, frowning when the puppy's sides heaved and he let out a dry, hacking cough. "His lungs sound pretty congested, too." She checked his chest with the stethoscope.

"Well?" Adam prompted.

Eva and Karl watched anxiously. They could tell by the look on their mother's face that she was worried.

"Bill's got the symptoms of something quite serious," she told Adam. "It wouldn't be covered by his first set of vaccinations for the parvo virus and so on. No—this is quite different."

"What is it?" Adam wanted the diagnosis, but Dr. Harrison wouldn't be rushed.

"The question is, where would Bill have picked it up?" she wondered. "If it is what I'm thinking, it would be highly infectious. But if it was at Joe Price's place . . . surely Joe would have let me know!"

"What is it, Mom?" Eva asked, suddenly afraid for poor little Bill. The gray-and-white speckled puppy lay on his side on the blue disinfected surface, hardly responding to her mom's thorough examination.

"I'm not totally sure." Heidi still wouldn't commit herself. She thought some more, then looked straight at Adam and made her diagnosis. "I think it *might* be kennel cough," she admitted at last. "And if it is, I'm afraid it's very bad news indeed."

Chapter Six

Karl went over to the computer and Googled "kennel cough." He read out his findings to Eva while their mom discussed Bill's treatment with Adam. "'Otherwise known as canine infectious tracheo-bronchitis.'"

"'Canine infectious trach...?" Eva echoed doubtfully, then trailed off.

"'Coughing localized to the windpipe and lungs. A respiratory disease caused by several different viruses or bacteria'."

"It sounds horrible!" Eva exclaimed. "Maybe we should put up a warning on the website? You know—'Watch out for kennel cough!'—so everyone realizes it's going around. How do dogs catch it?"

"They can pick it up in any number of places," their mom broke in as she came out of the examination room carrying Bill. "Dog shows, training classes, kennels—hence its common name, kennel cough. But in fact, they can catch it just by being taken for a walk in an area where another infected dog has been—like a park or a field. It's often impossible to track down the original culprit."

"But you think you can cure him?" Adam asked anxiously.

Heidi nodded and unlocked the medicine cabinet. "I hope he'll respond to these antibiotics. I'll also give you a spray that will open up his bronchial passages and help him to breathe more easily."

"Don't we have to keep him overnight?" Eva asked.

"No, but, Adam, you should keep Bill in complete isolation and change his bedding daily. Make sure the room where you keep him is well ventilated. And call me if you're worried."

"Even on Christmas Day?" the young farmer checked.

"In this job, we never close!" Heidi smiled as she opened the door and handed Bill over to his owner. "Merry Christmas!" she called to Adam. "And try not to be too concerned!"

"So where on earth did Bill pick up his infection?" Eva asked anxiously. "I'm sure he never even left Mr. Price's farm before being adopted, except to come here for his vaccinations!"

Heidi shook her head. "It's a mystery. Like I said, I'm certain Joe would have called me if any dog on his farm had contracted the virus. And he'd have known to keep the animal in strict isolation. This thing can last up to three months and it's very infectious. Most kennels won't take a dog in unless it's been vaccinated against kennel cough."

"And what happens if you don't treat it?" Karl wanted to know.

"There are all sorts of complications—permanent lung damage, for instance. And that can be life-threatening."

"You mean, Bill could die?" Eva asked.

"It's possible. But we've diagnosed it early and he's getting treatment. It's the dogs who never see a vet who suffer the most."

"So we should call Mr. Price and tell him about Bill right now," Karl suggested.

"Definitely." Heidi picked up the phone and dialed the number of Moorview Farm. "Hello, Joe? It's Heidi Harrison here . . ."

"And we'll have to call Mrs. Waterson," Eva remembered. "Mom, ask Mr. Price for Mrs. Waterson's address and phone number. We need to find out if Holly has caught the virus."

Her mom nodded. "Yes, Joe, that's right. Yes, I'm ninety-five percent sure it's kennel cough. Do me a favor and check Jess and the remaining puppies. . . . And can you give me the number for the people who bought Holly? . . . Oh, I see—yes, that's a problem. . . . No, I'll figure it out. Call me if you want me to come out and check on Jess, Ben, and Ivy—any time of day or night. Okay, yes, thanks."

"What's happened?" Eva asked as her mom put down the phone. She could tell from her mom's face that something was wrong.

"Joe doesn't have Mrs. Waterson's details anymore. After she picked up Holly he threw them away. He knows they came from 'town,' but isn't even sure which one."

"That's bad news," Karl muttered, shutting down the computer. "Now what are we going to do?"

Frantically, Eva thought back to the scene

in Joe Price's yard. She remembered how she'd run into the barn to collect first Holly and then Bill, leaving the other two pups safe in the cow stall. Then she recalled how Mrs. Waterson had opened her car door and let Lulu jump out and run all over the yard. "Mrs. Waterson said she couldn't get Lulu to do a thing she told her," she muttered to herself.

"What's that?" Karl asked.

"I said, Mrs. Waterson admitted that she had no control over Lulu, her Great Dane." It all came flooding back to Eva. "That was the reason she was on her way to take Lulu to the kennel for Christmas."

"Good memory, Eva!" Karl quickly saw how this would help. "Did she say which kennel?"

Eva shook her head. "But it must be somewhere nearby, because she said she was passing Moorview Farm on the way there, and there can't be that many boarding kennels around!"

"Here's a list," Heidi said, taking a piece of paper out of a desk drawer. "Nesfield Boarding Kennels and Okeham Cat and Dog Kennels are the most likely. Try them first, then go down the list. A Great Dane named Lulu shouldn't be too hard to track down!"

"Nesfield is a 'no,'" Karl reported after the first quick call. Time was ticking by. Before long, the offices at all the kennels would be closed and wouldn't open again until after Christmas.

"Okeham said no, too," Eva reported from the other telephone. "They said they didn't have any Watersons on their books, and no Great Danes, either."

"Okay, I'll try Ghyll Bank," Karl decided, picking up the phone again.

Eva's heart was starting to sink. "Hello, is this Low Lane Kennels?" she asked after she'd dialed a second number.

"Yes, but I'm afraid we're fully booked," the man's voice replied. "We did have one last-minute vacancy, but that was filled this afternoon."

"No, it's okay, I don't want to board a dog," Eva said quickly. "I'm calling from Animal Magic Rescue Center, trying to track down a Great Dane. I was wondering—do you have one named Lulu boarding with you?"

There was a pause before the voice replied. "That rings a bell. Let me check with my wife."

Eva held her breath and waited.

"Yes, I thought so." The man at Low Lane came back to the phone. "That's how our last-minute vacancy came up—a family named Waterson had booked their dog in over the phone. But when they turned up here, they had no vaccination certificates. The owner said she'd been too busy to get it done. And, of course, we don't take a dog unless the owner can produce the right paperwork. Anyway, I noticed the dog already had a watery discharge from her nose, plus a bit of a cough."

"So what happened?" Eva asked, hanging on the man's every word.

"We turned them away."

"So Mrs. Waterson took Lulu home?"

"That's right. To be honest, the dog looked like a bit of a handful. I didn't envy the little Border collie pup she had with her."

Eva's heart rate quickened as she asked the kennel owner one last question. "Please, can you give me the Watersons' address and telephone number?"

There was another long pause before the man replied. "Sorry," he reported back. "My wife erased their information off the computer."

Chapter Seven

"Look—it's snowing!" Eva's dad told her after dinner. He led her to the kitchen window and made her look outside. "It's like a real-life Christmas card!"

Eva watched big white flakes float down from the dark sky. Already the yard and the rescue center roof were covered in a thick layer of snow.

"Why the sad face on Christmas Eve?" her dad asked gently. "Do you want to tell me what's up?"

"No thanks, Dad. I'm okay."

"No, you're not," he insisted, drawing her toward the log fire. Eva's mom and Karl were in the living room, stacking presents under the house Christmas tree. "Come on—spill the beans!"

"I can't help worrying about Holly," Eva confessed. Once she'd started, the whole story tumbled out. "Puppies can die from kennel cough," she ended up breathlessly. "And you know something—I bet Todd Waterson and his mom won't know what to do if Holly gets sick!"

"You can't say that for sure," her dad warned. "Listen, Eva, I know this is hard for you, but it may be something we can't do anything about. Without knowing which town the Watersons live in, we might just have to let the problem go."

Eva's eyes filled with tears. "But this is their

fault. I'm sure Lulu is the one who's infecting the others—the man at Low Lane Kennels said she had a runny nose and a bad cough."

Her dad sighed. "We still can't help, however much we might want to."

Eva nodded as a tear splashed onto her cheek.

"So we just have to accept that Holly and Lulu have disappeared and concentrate on enjoying Christmas, okay?"

This time Eva couldn't even manage a nod. Instead, she sniffed, then said, "I'm going out to check the cat kennels and say hi to Lottie."

"Good idea," her dad agreed. "Put your jacket on. It's cold out there."

Eva found the lot cat curled up and asleep in her warm bed. "You look snug," she whispered.

At the sound of Eva's voice, Lottie opened her eyes.

"Sorry, I didn't mean to wake you!" Eva leaned into the unit and stroked the thin cat. "Look at your fur—it's all spiky and uneven."

Meow! Lottie stood up and brushed against Eva's hand for another stroke.

"There! You're so cute. How did you end

up in an empty lot?"

Meow! Lottie said again.

"Never mind, after Christmas we're going to find you a lovely home with a nice, kind person to take really good care of you," Eva promised.

Nearby, other cats meowed for attention so Eva went down the row, stroking them and talking gently. Then, after ten minutes, she decided it was time to go back to the house. "I'll try to be more cheerful!" she promised Lottie as she took one last look. "After all, it's not fair to ruin everyone's Christmas, is it?"

Meow! Lottie replied, settling down to sleep again.

Eva left the cat kennels and quietly closed the door. She turned up the collar of her jacket and stepped out into the snowy yard. Farther along Main Street, she heard the sound of carolers.

"Deck the halls with boughs of holly . . . "

Eva walked across the yard, gazing up at the whirling, ice-cold flakes. Suddenly, she heard footsteps around the front of the house. "Who's that?" she wondered.

Perhaps it was one of the carolers running ahead of the others to knock on doors. She went around the side to take a look, but there was no one there.

"That's funny," Eva muttered, spotting scuff marks and footprints in the snow. The footsteps headed to and from the front doorstep. "Weird."

She looked up and down the street—no, definitely no one there. Then she turned and stopped dead.

There was a small, dark shape on the doorstep. Eva stepped closer to take a look.

The shape moved—a small creature, half covered in snow. She looked again.

"Yip!" the tiny thing cried.

At first Eva couldn't believe what she was seeing. A black-and-white puppy with speckled front legs was shivering and crying on the doorstep.

"Holly?" Eva whispered.

The collie pup gave another tiny bark.

"Oh, Holly!" Eva gasped, picking her up and knocking frantically on her own front door. "Mom, Dad, Karl, open the door quick! It's Holly—she's been abandoned on our doorstep. Quick, before she freezes to death!"

"I'll keep her warm by the fire while you run for the medicine and equipment you need," Eva's dad said to her mom.

Karl had opened the door and let Eva and Holly in, then the whole family sprang into action. "Yes, we can't take her anywhere near the other dogs," Heidi agreed. "She probably has kennel cough, just like Bill. We'll have to isolate her until the infection is dealt with."

Eva's mom ran across to the office while Eva gave her dad a towel to dry the melting snow from a still-shivering Holly.

"I'm going out to look for the person who dumped her," Karl decided, grabbing his jacket. He left by the front door and ran up Main Street.

"Maybe she found her own way here," Eva's dad suggested after Karl had left.

But Eva shook her head. "I heard footsteps. There were tracks in the snow." She stood to one side as her mom dashed back in and got to work.

"The same symptoms as Bill's," Dr. Harrison muttered after she'd listened to Holly's chest. "And this time there's a discharge from her eyes."

Eva's heart beat fast, but she tried not to panic. "Don't worry, Holly," she whispered, crouching down to stroke her favorite puppy. "Mom knows what she's doing. She's a really good vet!"

Poor Holly gazed up at Eva with a scared

look in her dark brown eyes.

Eva stroked her gently. "Now that you're here at Animal Magic, you'll be safe. I won't leave you until you're better, cross my heart!"

Chapter Eight

"It's a total mystery," Karl reported. He'd been up and down Main Street, quizzing the carolers and other passersby. "Nobody saw anything unusual—no cars pulling up outside our house, no strangers—nothing!"

"Just dumped!" Eva said angrily. "How cruel is that!"

"Shh." Eva's mom had finished treating Holly and now appealed for everyone to be calm. "What's done is done. The main thing is that she is receiving good care."

"Poor Holly," Eva sighed, afraid to pick her up yet longing to cuddle her. The puppy lay on a big cushion, soaking up the heat from the log fire.

Holly took a short breath, then let out a noisy, dry cough. She coughed for so long that Eva was scared she had something stuck in her throat.

"She sounds awful," Karl muttered.

"Yes, but the antibiotics will kick in soon," their mom told them. "And I'm thinking an old-fashioned remedy might help, too."

"What is it?" Eva said eagerly. She would do anything to help Holly.

"Bring her upstairs. We'll run a hot shower and close the bathroom door. We'll keep Holly in there for twenty minutes so she can inhale the steam. That'll ease the cough."

"Like a sauna," Karl realized as Eva carried the puppy upstairs.

"I'll sit with her," Eva offered.

And so all through the rest of Christmas Eve, Eva kept her promise not to leave Holly on her own—first in the steam-filled bathroom, then down in the kitchen again, settling her back on her comfy cushion and gently patting the tiny puppy's chest as her mom had showed her.

"That's called coupage," Eva's mom

explained. "It's another way of helping the cough."

"I think it's working," Karl said. "She seems better already."

By bedtime, Eva had made a decision. "I'm not going to bed tonight," she announced. "I'll stay down here and sleep in a sleeping bag next to Holly."

Her dad smiled. "Don't forget to bring your Christmas stocking down with you. And I'd better let Santa know that you're camping downstairs!"

"Da-ad!" Eva groaned.

"It's okay, I'll get your sleeping bag and pajamas." Her mom laughed. "And we'll find the air mattress for you. Come on, let's get organized. It's late and I don't know about anyone else, but I'm exhausted."

Fifteen minutes later, Eva snuggled down in her sleeping bag beside Holly, making sure she could see her in the dim light of the dying fire. "Don't worry," she whispered as her mom checked the fireguard, turned off the light, and closed the door. "Everything's going to be all right—I promise!"

Outside, the snow kept falling. By midnight all of Okeham was sparkling and silent. Then the sky cleared. Stars shone and dawn crept in with a faint pink light.

Eva woke to the sound of Holly whimpering. "What is it?" she whispered, wondering at first where she was, then realizing she was on a mattress on the kitchen floor. The empty Christmas stocking, which her dad had hung from the back of a chair, was now stuffed with brightly wrapped presents.

The little puppy sat up on her cushion, ears pricked. She gave a sharp yap.

"It's okay, I'm still here," Eva whispered, surprised that she'd managed to sleep at all. The last thing she remembered was drowsily gazing at Holly, who was asleep on her cushion. Now it was almost light—it was Christmas Day!

Holly barked again.

"Shh!"

"Yip! Yap!" The puppy slid off her cushion and ran to the door.

"Hey, you must really be feeling better!" Eva exclaimed. "But what's bothering you?" Sleepily, Eva struggled out of her sleeping bag and followed Holly. She peered through the window at the snowy yard. "Oh!" she gasped, frozen to the spot with shock.

A small, worried face was peering back at her. The face was full of fear as its eyes met Eva's.

"Todd?"

In an instant, the face had vanished. Eva hurriedly unlocked the door. She ran out in her bare feet, just in time to see Todd Waterson sprinting away.

"Please let me follow him!" Eva begged. She was back in the kitchen, shoving her feet into her boots and flinging her jacket on over her pajamas. "Mom, I have to go!"

Eva's mom had heard the kitchen door open and came downstairs to investigate. "Follow who? Eva, hang on a minute—tell me exactly what happened!"

"Todd Waterson—he was here a few seconds ago, peeping through the window!"

"Are you sure you weren't dreaming?"

"No, Holly heard him creeping around outside. She started to bark. That's why I woke up." Seconds were slipping by. Todd was getting away clean.

"But what was he doing here at this time of the morning? How did he get here?" To Eva's mom none of this made sense. She stood in front of the door, blocking Eva's way out.

"All I know is—he was here!"

"What's going on?" Karl mumbled, appearing at the foot of the stairs, his hair messed up, his face still bleary with sleep.

"Karl, get dressed!" Eva cried. "You have to help me find Todd. He was just here, obviously looking for Holly."

"You mean, he's the one who dumped her?" Karl asked.

Eva nodded. "How else would he know she was here?"

"Merry Christmas, everyone." It was their dad's turn to interrupt. He'd followed Karl downstairs, still half-asleep. "Is it time to open presents?"

"Merry Christmas, Dad," Eva babbled. She was desperate to follow Todd, but her hopes of finding him were fading. "Karl, hurry up—Todd's getting away!"

"Eva says she saw Todd Waterson snooping around the house," her mom explained to her dad. "I know, I'm surprised, too. But I suppose we have to let Karl and Eva take a look."

Her dad nodded.

"Hurray!" *At last!* Eva hurried across to Holly to explain. "We won't be long. You have to wait here where it's nice and warm. Mom says you have to rest as much as possible!"

Holly wagged her little tail.

"Stay!" Eva held up a warning finger. "I'll see you in a bit—okay!"

Chapter Nine

"So which way did Todd go?" Karl wondered as he and Eva stepped out into the first light of Christmas Day.

"That's easy—he went past Annie's house!" Eva pointed to one set of clear footprints—the only ones to spoil the smooth covering of snow.

"Let's go!" Karl cried. "If we hurry, we can catch up to him."

"He looked pretty scared when he saw

me," Eva said. "He'll be running as fast as he can."

"Look here—a skid mark—he must have slipped."

"And here's another one." Eva pointed to where Todd's footprints turned down a side street and headed downhill. Her own feet crunched into the crisp snow. "Whoa!" she cried, grabbing onto a gatepost as she slid and almost fell.

"The trail is leading us to Riverview Road," Karl pointed out. "I wonder who Todd Waterson knows down here."

Eva shrugged. It was weird being out so early, when all her friends would be jumping out of warm beds and tearing at wrapping paper to see what Santa Claus had brought. "Let's go find out," she said, following Todd's tracks to the short row of terraced houses overlooking the river. The trail led into the yard of number four.

"Are we going to knock on the door?" Karl asked. "Won't it look a bit—weird?"

"Who cares?" Eva replied. "All that matters is finding out why Todd dumped Holly on our doorstep!"

She knocked loudly on the red door and waited.

After a while, there was the sound of someone unlatching the lock, and a woman's head appeared. "Yes?" she asked warily. She was in her bathrobe, with white terry-cloth slippers on her feet.

"Sorry to bother you," Eva said, trying to peer down the hallway. "We're looking for Todd Waterson."

"He's in bed," the woman answered. "Anyway—do you have any idea what time it is?"

Just then, a second woman appeared in

the corridor. Eva recognized her right away as Todd's mother. "We definitely got the right place!" she muttered to Karl, who was hanging back and looking embarrassed. "Mrs. Waterson, we need to speak to Todd!"

"As my sister said, Todd's still asleep," Mrs. Waterson insisted. "What's this all about?"

"Are you sure he's in bed?" Eva stood her ground. "I think you'd better check."

"Look here!" Mrs. Waterson stepped out onto the porch. "I've seen you before—up at Moorview Farm."

Eva nodded. "My mom and dad run Animal Magic Rescue Center. Mom did Holly's vaccinations."

"So you're here to check up on Holly when you should be at home with your family, enjoying Christmas like everyone else. I think I'd better speak to your parents."

"I'm going to check on Todd," her sister decided, then disappeared upstairs.

"If you must know, I left Lulu and Holly at home," Andrea Waterson told Eva with a hostile stare. "A neighbor is popping in to check on them while we're away."

"But you can't do that, even if it was true!" Eva cried. "Holly has only been with you a couple of days. She's just a puppy. It's not fair to leave her alone like that!"

"But it's *not* true." Karl stepped forward with the facts. "Because we've got Holly at Animal Magic."

"That's not possible!" Mrs. Waterson gasped.

Her sister ran downstairs in a panic. "Andrea, Todd isn't in his bed!"

Mrs. Waterson's hands flew to her face.

"It's been slept in, but he isn't there now!" Todd's aunt confirmed. She looked hard at Eva. "Tell us what's going on!"

"That's what we're trying to find out!" Eva muttered. "Todd was at our place just a few minutes ago, peering in through the window—we followed his trail back here."

"It's obvious he snuck out," Karl said thoughtfully as Andrea Waterson and her sister started to panic. "And the tracks show that he definitely came back. I reckon he's hiding somewhere close by because he's scared. . . ."

"Scared of what?" Mrs. Waterson interrupted. "Oh, this is terrible!"

"Wait a second!" Eva's sharp eyes had spotted a trail of water across the hallway tiles. It led to a closet under the stairs. "That could be melted snow from Todd's boots."

In an instant, Andrea Waterson had dashed down the hall and flung open the low door. "Oh, Todd—there you are!" she cried, dragging him out. "Oh, poor boy— you're shivering. What on earth have you been doing?"

Eva and Karl sat at Todd's aunt's kitchen table, waiting for him to explain everything. Todd was crying, even though his mom had hugged him and told him over and over that he wasn't in trouble, whatever he'd done. "But you have to tell us what happened," she insisted gently. "How did Holly arrive on Karl and Eva's doorstep?"

"You won't be angry with me?" Todd whispered nervously.

His mom held his hand and shook her head. "Of course not."

"Okay. I did it because Holly was sick," Todd confessed.

"Did what?" His aunt Fiona gave everyone a mug of hot chocolate, then sat down at the table to listen.

"I smuggled Holly out of our house in a big bag of Christmas presents—because she wasn't very well and I didn't want to leave her all alone."

"Holly would have been perfectly okay with Mrs. Browning looking after her. . . ." Mrs. Waterson began. Then she blushed and fell silent.

"You didn't even realize that Lulu was sick," Todd went on. "I tried to tell you, but you were too busy to listen."

"So then what happened?" Eva prompted. "After you smuggled Holly out in the bag of presents, what then?"

"Mom drove here to Aunt Fiona's and I sneaked Holly upstairs. But she was really sick now—coughing and sniffling—and I was scared."

"So you snuck out and brought her to Animal Magic," Karl concluded.

Todd nodded. "I'd seen the sign outside the rescue center when we drove past. I left Holly on the doorstep because I needed you to look after her."

"It would've been better to knock on the door," Eva told him. "As it was, it was lucky we found her."

Todd hung his head. "I was going to, then I heard you walking across the yard and I was scared. Really scared. So I ran away. Is Holly okay?" he asked, wiping tears from his face with the back of his hand. "Is she getting better?"

"Slowly," Eva told him. "She's got kennel cough. Mom's given her some medicine, but it'll take a while for Holly to get completely better."

"But you definitely did the right thing, Todd," Karl added. "If you hadn't brought her to Animal Magic, she might have died."

At this, Andrea Waterson sprang to her own defense. "I couldn't bring the dogs here, could I?" she appealed to her sister. "There isn't room for Lulu in this tiny

107

house. Besides, it was only for a couple of days."

"And you didn't realize they were sick." Fiona tried to help, but it only seemed to make her sister feel worse.

Mrs. Waterson turned to Eva. "What about Lulu?" she asked quietly. "Does she have this kennel cough, too?"

"We think she's the one who had it first, and she passed it on to Holly and Bill," Eva replied before turning to her brother. "Karl, what are we going to do about Lulu?"

"We'll tell Mom," he decided quickly. "Mrs. Waterson, will you lend us your house key? Dad will be able to drive over and bring Lulu back to the rescue center. But if we're going to help Lulu, we have to do it now—before presents, or breakfast, or anything!"

Chapter Ten

"See how well Holly's doing," Eva said as she led Todd into the kitchen at Animal Magic. "She's almost back to normal!"

The puppy stood up and wagged her tail.

Todd heaved a sigh of relief. "Hi, Holly. It's me!" He turned to Eva. "Can I pick her up?"

She nodded. Through the open door, she could hear Mrs. Waterson talking to her mom.

"You can cuddle her, but don't let her get too excited," Eva warned Todd before she tuned in to the conversation in the living room.

"Mark and Karl shouldn't be too long, snow permitting," Eva's mom was saying to Todd's mom. "The sooner they get back here with Lulu, the better. If she's already had this infection for a number of days, there may be secondary problems that need to be looked at as soon as possible."

"I see now that I've been terribly irresponsible," Mrs. Waterson said after a long pause. "But the truth is—I've been very busy trying to organize Christmas without my husband."

"That's okay," Heidi said kindly. "You don't have to explain."

"I'm sorry I've made such a mess of looking after the dogs."

Heidi nodded. "Like we always say—people must think long and hard about having pets if they're going to feel tied down by them over holiday periods."

"I'm afraid that's true for us—given that we own the house in Spain. I didn't really think things through when I gave in to Gina's pressure for us to have a dog. As for buying Holly for Todd—it was more my idea than his. I thought he'd like to have a puppy, like his sister does."

"Listen, I can hear Mark's van in the yard." Eva's mom cut the conversation short. "If you'll excuse me . . . !"

Hearing this, Eva peered through the window. "Here comes Dad!" she told Todd, leaving Holly with him and his mom and dashing outside. "Do you have Lulu?" she asked Karl, who jumped out of the van first.

He nodded. "She's in bad shape—she's

gone downhill really fast since last night when the neighbor went in to feed her."

"That's what happens with this illness," their mom said. She reminded her husband and Karl to keep Lulu away from the kennels as they lifted the sick Great Dane out of the van. "Best to carry her into the empty stable block. We'll keep her isolated and make a bed for her there."

Quickly, the arrangements were made. While Heidi went to get antibiotics and an IV, Eva ran ahead into the stables to arrange a bed of straw covered by a clean horse blanket from the tack room. Eva's dad and Karl laid her down gently.

"She's wheezing badly," Mark warned his wife when she came back. "And she's hardly got the energy to stand, let alone walk."

Nodding, Eva's mom began her treatment. "The problem here is that there's an organism called mycoplasma involved— a hybrid of both a virus and a bacterium— which means that the antibiotic isn't foolproof."

Once more, Eva was caught by a sudden rush of worry. She knelt down by Lulu and stroked her softly.

The Great Dane slowly raised her head and nuzzled Eva's hand.

"Let's hope Lulu's immune system is strong enough to kick in and fight back," Eva's mom said, standing back at last. She and Eva's dad made way for Todd and his mother, who had just come into the stable to see Lulu.

They all gazed down at the patient.

"How is she?" Mrs. Waterson asked.

"She's doing okay," Heidi replied. "You can stay with her for a while, if you like."

Todd nodded. He knelt in the straw and stroked Lulu.

"We'll be in the kitchen if you need us," Eva's dad assured the Watersons, leading his wife, Karl, and Eva out of the stable and closing the door.

Back in the house, Eva grew thoughtful. "Mom, if Holly and Lulu do get better, will they have to go back to the Watersons?"

"Yes, wouldn't it be better if we put the dogs on our website and found new owners who could look after them properly?" Karl argued eagerly.

Their mom glanced out across the snowy yard. "Lulu and Holly haven't been signed over to us," she pointed out.

Their dad agreed. "At Animal Magic, we

can't take in pets without their owners' permission."

"True," Karl admitted.

Eva wasn't convinced. All she could think about was Lulu and adorable Holly. "But the Watersons aren't very good with animals. Holly's been through a lot already—I'd hate to think what else could go wrong!"

"Let's talk about it later," her mom warned as she looked out of the window and saw Todd and his mom appear at the stable door.

Eva sighed loudly.

"At least we can give Mrs. Waterson the name of a good dog trainer," her dad suggested. "Then, when Lulu and Holly get better, we'll know they have access to the best possible teacher."

"Hmm," Dr. Harrison said slowly. She seemed to be deep in thought.

"I bet Mrs. Waterson will agree to do that,"

Karl said. "She seems pretty sorry about what happened."

Eva's mom patted Eva's arm as the Watersons walked across the yard toward the house. "Mark, let's have a quick word," she suggested. "Wait here," she told Eva and Karl, swiftly taking their dad outside.

"What's going on?" Eva wondered.

Karl listened at the door. "I can't hear a word," he told her, going to the window instead. "All I can tell you is that Mom and Dad have finished talking and decided to intercept the Watersons!"

"I'm still worried, Karl. I wish we could wave a magic wand and change the Watersons into perfect dog owners!"

"If only!" He sighed.

Together they watched their mom and dad having a long talk with Mrs. Waterson. Todd listened quietly, nodding whenever his mom turned to ask him a question. He waited patiently as she took out her cellphone and made a long call. Then at last, Todd and his mother walked with Eva's parents toward the house.

"Karl and Eva, Todd has something to say to you," Mrs. Waterson announced as all four came into the kitchen.

Eva held Holly safe in her arms, feeling her rough pink tongue lick her fingers.

"Thank you for saving Holly," Todd began.

"And thank you!" Eva said softly. "Bringing her here to Okeham with you was what really saved her life."

Todd swallowed hard. "Your mom and dad and my mom have been talking about Holly and Lulu," he went on. "Mom's decided that it would be best to put Lulu on the Animal Magic website."

"You mean—you want us to find her a new home?" Eva gasped. She guessed that Todd was bravely holding back the tears. "And do you think so, too?"

He nodded. "We called Dad and Gina and they agreed that we weren't looking after Lulu very well."

"She needs a house with a bigger yard and someone who can take her for long walks," Mrs. Waterson explained.

"When she gets better, can you find her somewhere like that?" Todd asked Eva and Karl.

"You bet!" Karl said quickly, while Eva stared at Todd in surprise.

"Ssshh, stay still, Holly!" she murmured as the puppy wriggled on her lap.

"And what else, Todd?" his mother prompted.

"We haven't looked after Holly very well, either," he said miserably. "She was having a lovely time with her brothers and sister at Moorview Farm, and ever since she came to our house she's been sad."

"Wait! What are you saying?" Eva gasped. She glanced at her mom and dad, who had on their secretive, "Don't ask us!" expressions.

"Do you mean you want us to find a new

home for Holly, too?" Karl asked excitedly. "A home in the country, where she has space to run around and herd sheep and do real sheepdog things?"

There was a long pause while Eva held tightly to precious Holly.

"Not exactly," Todd said with a frown.

"What, then?" Eva asked, leaping up.

Todd came to stand close to her and the puppy. "We'd like you to keep Holly," he murmured.

"Me?" Eva said faintly.

"You and Karl," her dad said, watching her face slowly light up. "Your mom and I talked it through, and we both agreed to break our golden rule of no family pets."

"Just this once!" their mom warned. "Since you're so fond of Holly and this is a very special case."

Eva went over to Karl. "Did you hear that?" she said excitedly.

Karl took the puppy in his arms. He nodded.

"Karl's too happy to speak!" Their dad laughed. "So, what about you, Eva? Do you think it's a good idea?"

"Pinch me, somebody, and tell me it's true!" she cried. She beamed at Todd. "Don't worry—Holly will live here with us and you can come see her whenever you want!"

"How about right after Christmas dinner?"

Mr. Harrison suggested with a wink.

Todd nodded eagerly. He watched Karl set Holly down on her cushion by the fire, then looked out across the yard, past the stables to the fields beyond. "She's going to love it here, isn't she, Mom?"

"Definitely," Mrs. Waterson agreed. Then quietly she took Todd's hand and led him toward the car.

"This is the *best* Christmas ever!" Eva cried.

The turkey was roasting in the oven, the presents were opened, and wrapping paper lay scattered over the kitchen floor.

Karl laughed as Holly got tangled up in red ribbon, then pounced on Eva.

"Merry Christmas, everyone!" their granddad called as he opened the door and kicked off his snowy boots. There was an inviting smell of Christmas dinner, newly opened presents . . . and chaos in the kitchen. "Good heavens, what's going on here?"

Eva flew to greet him. "Granddad, guess what's happened!"

"Has Santa paid you a visit?" he asked with a twinkle in his eye.

"Better than that," Karl said, a grin spreading from ear to ear.

From under a large piece of silver

wrapping paper, Holly made a sudden
pounce at their granddad's feet. She
growled and crouched down, ready to
attack his thick gray socks.

"Mom and Dad have broken their rule!"
Eva cried, swooping to pick Holly up and
cuddle her. She and Karl had a puppy of
their very own—it was a dream come true.
"Holly is going to live at Animal Magic.
She's ours—to keep!"

Collect all the books in the series!

Visit the Animal Magic website:
www.animalmagicrescue.net

THE PUPPY PLACE

SO MANY PERFECT PUPPIES - COLLECT THEM ALL!

GOLDIE

SNOWBALL

SHADOW

RASCAL

BUDDY

FLASH

SCOUT

PATCHES

PUGSLEY

MAGGIE and MAX

NOODLE

PRINCESS

CODY

BEAR

HONEY

LUCKY